JOHN BURNINGHAM

Would You Rather...

SeaStar Books

NEW YORK

SEASTAR BOOKS
A division of NORTH-SOUTH BOOKS INC.

Published in the United States in 2002 by SeaStar Books, a division of
North-South Books Inc., New York.

Library of Congress Cataloging-in-Publication Data is available.

ISBN 1-58717-135-X (reinforced trade edition)
1 3 5 7 9 RTE 10 8 6 4 2

Printed in Singapore

For more information about our books, and the authors and artists who
create them, visit our web site: www.northsouth.com

Would you rather . . .

your **HOUSE** were surrounded by

WATER

SNOW

or **JUNGLE**?

Would you rather . . .

an **ELEPHANT** drank your **BATHWATER**

an **EAGLE** stole your **DINNER**

a **PIG** tried on your **CLOTHES**

or a **HIPPO** slept in your **BED**?

Would you rather be . . .

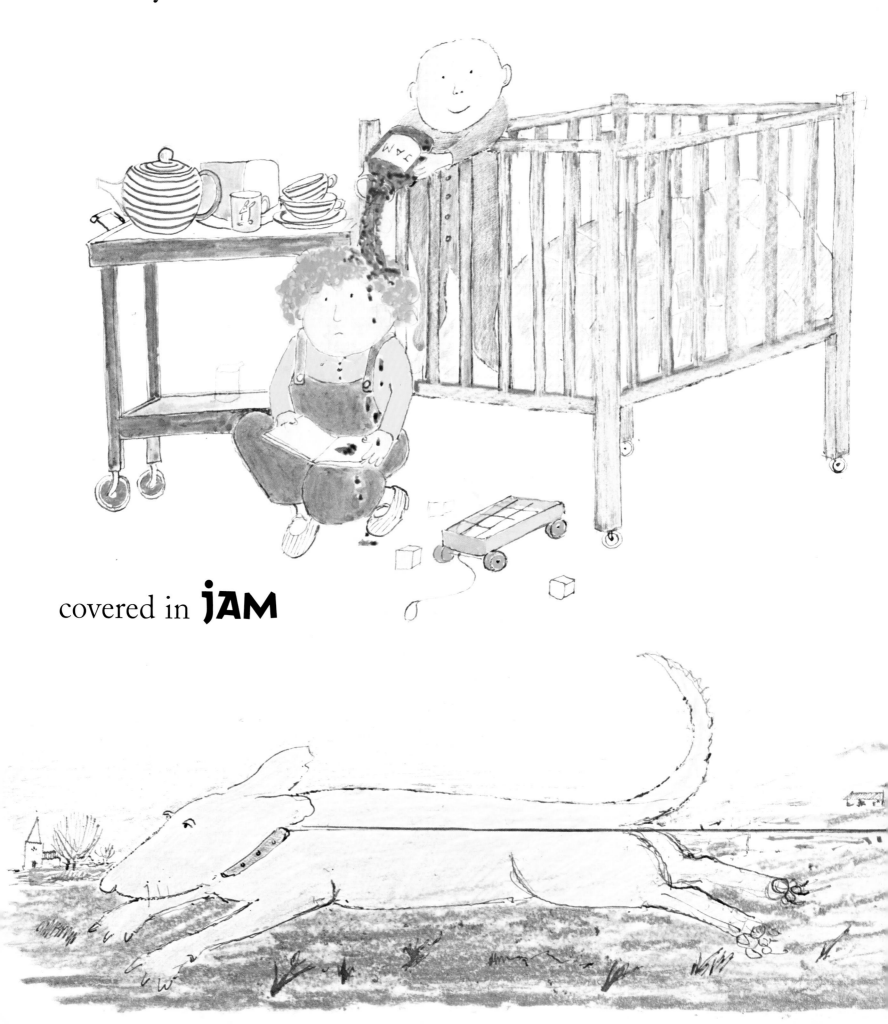

covered in **jAM**

SOAKED

with water

or pulled through the **MUD** by a dog?

Would you rather have . . .

supper in a **CASTLE**

breakfast in a **BALLOON**

or tea on the **RIVER**?

Would you rather be made to . . .

eat **SPIDER** stew

taste **SLUG** dumplings

chew mashed **WORMS**

or drink a **SNAIL** shake?

Would you rather . . .

JUMP in the **NETTLES** for five dollars

SWALLOW a dead **FROG** for twenty dollars

or stay all night in a
CREEPY HOUSE
for fifty dollars?

Would you rather be . . .

CRUSHED by a **SNAKE**

SWALLOWED by a **FISH**

EATEN by a **CROCODILE**

or **SAT ON** by a **RHINOCEROS**?

Would you rather . . .

your **DAD** did a **DANCE** at school

or your **MOM** made a **FUSS** in a café?

Would you rather . . .

CLASH two cymbals

BANG a drum

or **BLOW** a trumpet?

Would you rather . . .

TiCKLE a monkey

READ to a koala

BOX with a cat

SKATE with a dog

RIDE on a pig

or **DANCE** with a goat?

Would you rather be **CHASED** by . . .

a **CRAB**

a **BULL**

a **LION**

or **WOLVES**?

Or would you like to
RiDE a **BULL**
into a supermarket?

Would you rather be **LOST** . . .

in the **FOG**

at **SEA**

in a **DESERT**

in a **FOREST**

or in a **CROWD**?

Would you rather help . . .

a **FAIRY** make magic

GNOMES dig for treasure

an **IMP** be naughty

a **WITCH** make stew

or **SANTA CLAUS** deliver presents?

Would you rather live with . . .

a **GERBIL** in a cage

a **FISH** in a bowl

a **PARROT** on a perch

a **RABBIT** in a hutch

CHICKENS in a coop

or a **DOG** in a kennel?

Or perhaps you would rather
just go to sleep in
YOUR OWN BED!